THIS IS MY FAMILY

BY GINA AND MERCER MAYER

A GOLDEN BOOK • NEW YORK

Golden Books Publishing Company, Inc., Racine, Wisconsin 53404

This is my family.
We live together.

Sometimes we fight, but mostly we have fun. I think my family is special.

This is my dad. He works in an office so that he can buy us things.

Sometimes we go to visit him there.
He lets me play on the computer.
But I have to be careful not to push
the wrong buttons.

When Dad comes home from the office, he likes to play catch with me.

But sometimes he's too tired.

This is my mom. She takes care of all of us.

She keeps our house nice and neat.

She makes sure we have clean clothes to wear.

And when we're sick, she sits up with
us all night, even if she's sleepy.

And when I hurt myself, she always
makes me feel better.

This is my sister. She's not so bad.

When I don't have anything to do,
I play with her. We have a good time,
but sometimes she hurts my toys.

I think my sister likes me a lot
because she always wants to tag along
with me.

This is my baby brother. He's cute, but he's not too much fun.

I have to be quiet when he sleeps.

And sometimes he cries at night
and wakes me up.
Then I get scared.

Sometimes Mom lets me hold my brother. He's real soft. I like it when he smiles at me.

These are my pets. They are part of
my family, too.

My sister likes
to dress our cat
in doll clothes.
I don't think he
likes that too much.

My dog likes to chase the ball
when I play catch. Sometimes
he won't give it back.

My goldfish doesn't do anything
but swim around. I think he's bored,
but Mom won't let him take a bath
with me.

This is me. I try to be a good critter, most of the time.

I help my dad work in the yard.

Sometimes I take out
the garbage for him.

I set the table for Mom, and I help her
fold the clean clothes.

I try not to make my sister cry too much, and I push my baby brother around in his stroller.

This is my family. Each one of us is different, but we love each other a lot.

I think that's what a family is all about.